HOW YOUR BODY WORKS

Judy Hindley
assisted by Christopher Rawson

Illustrated by Colin King
Designed by John Jamieson and Geoff Davis

Medical Adviser: Susan Jenkins, MRCP, DCH
Educational Adviser: Paula Varrow

First published in 1975
Usborne Publishing Ltd
Usborne House
83-85 Saffron Hill
London EC1N 8RT
© Usborne Publishing Ltd 1992, 1975

The name Usborne and the device are
Trade Marks of Usborne Publishing Ltd.

Printed in Belgium UE

About This Book

In many ways, your body is like a marvellous machine. It can do hundreds of different kinds of jobs. To show how it does some of its most important jobs, we have invented lots of different machines.

Our machines do not connect with each other. Each is separate, and each can do only some of the jobs your body can do.

For example, our Eating Machine (pages 4 and 5) shows what your body does to food after you swallow it.

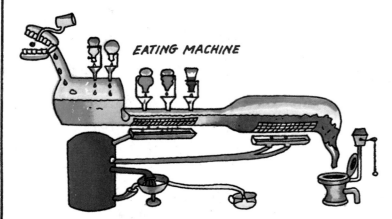

EATING MACHINE

Our Teeth-and-Tongue Machine (pages 6 and 7) is a completely separate machine. We made it to show what different teeth do.

TEETH AND TONGUE MACHINE

Our Breathing Machine (pages 12 and 13) shows how your ribs work with a special muscle to make you breathe.

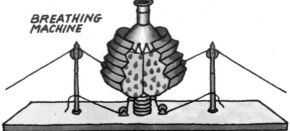

BREATHING MACHINE

We made up a mechanical man (pages 28 to 31) so that we could show how other muscles work to move your bones.

MECHANICAL MAN

Real machines are much better than bodies at doing some things. Computers can calculate faster. Cranes can lift heavier loads. Cars can move faster.

But your body fits together so well that it can do many different jobs — and it can do lots of them at the same time.

No scientist has ever been able to make a machine as neat and light as your body that could do even half the things your body does. And no machine can have new ideas, or make jokes, or change its mind — or have babies.

How Your Body Works

Contents

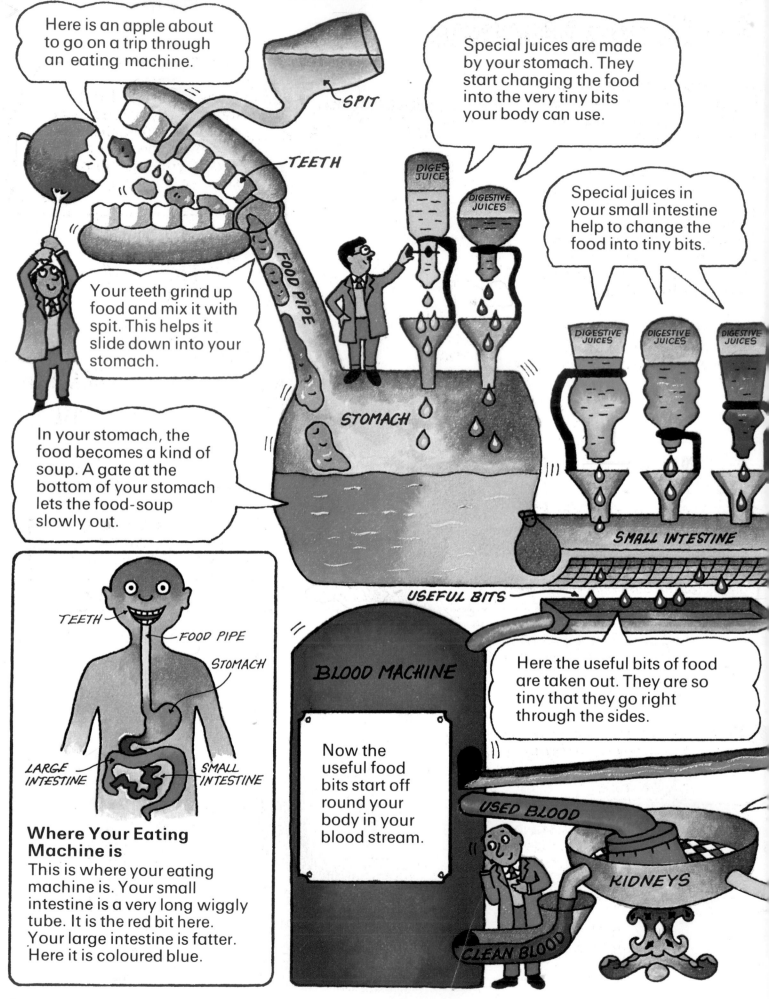

Here is an apple about to go on a trip through an eating machine.

SPIT

TEETH

Special juices are made by your stomach. They start changing the food into the very tiny bits your body can use.

Special juices in your small intestine help to change the food into tiny bits.

Your teeth grind up food and mix it with spit. This helps it slide down into your stomach.

FOOD PIPE

DIGESTIVE JUICES

DIGESTIVE JUICES

DIGESTIVE JUICES   DIGESTIVE JUICES   DIGESTIVE JUICES

STOMACH

In your stomach, the food becomes a kind of soup. A gate at the bottom of your stomach lets the food-soup slowly out.

SMALL INTESTINE

USEFUL BITS

TEETH

FOOD PIPE

STOMACH

LARGE INTESTINE

SMALL INTESTINE

Where Your Eating Machine is

This is where your eating machine is. Your small intestine is a very long wiggly tube. It is the red bit here. Your large intestine is fatter. Here it is coloured blue.

BLOOD MACHINE

Here the useful bits of food are taken out. They are so tiny that they go right through the sides.

Now the useful food bits start off round your body in your blood stream.

USED BLOOD

KIDNEYS

CLEAN BLOOD

4

An Eating Machine

Here is a machine we have invented that shows the main things that happen to the food you eat.

In your food there are things your body can use and things it cannot use. In your eating machine, the food is chopped and churned and changed into tiny bits by special juices. This is called digestion.

Then the useful things can be sorted out and sent where they are needed.

To get rid of bad food, muscles in your chest and near your stomach squeeze together. The gate at the end of your stomach stays shut, so the food goes up.

CHEST SQUEEZES DOWN

Stomach juices mixed with the food make it taste sour.

MUSCLE SQUEEZES UP

GATE STAYS SHUT

LARGE INTESTINE

The rubbish is very sludgy by the time it gets here. You get rid of it when you go to the lavatory.

WATER

Water is taken out here. It goes right through the sides. It becomes part of your blood.

Used blood goes to the kidneys to be cleaned. Clean blood goes back into the blood stream. The waste water goes into the lavatory.

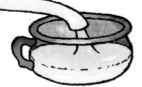

5

A Teeth-and-Tongue Machine

This teeth-and-tongue machine gets food ready to be swallowed. It does the main things your teeth and tongue do.

This machine has a chopper and some grinding wheels. You have special kinds of teeth to do what these parts do. Below you can see how they look.

Your front teeth have sharp edges to chop off bites.

CHOPPER

SPIT

TONGUE

Your tongue carries food to your grinders. It takes the mashed-up bites to the back of your throat when you swallow.

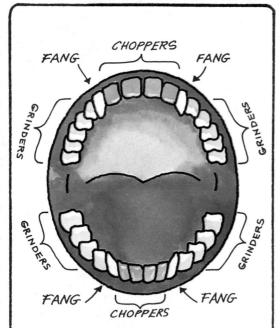

Count the Teeth
After your first teeth fall out, you will grow 32 big teeth. Your jaw has to grow too, so they fit in. This picture shows how many of each kind will grow.

FANG CHOPPERS FANG
GRINDERS GRINDERS
GRINDERS GRINDERS
FANG CHOPPERS FANG

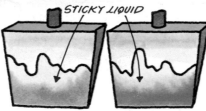

STICKY LIQUID

Why do Teeth go Bad ?
Liquid from chewed food sticks to your teeth. You cannot see this. But if you slide your tongue round your teeth, they may feel gluey.

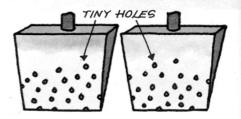

TINY HOLES

If the stickiness stays, it makes tiny holes in your teeth. This is a bit like the rust you get on metal tools when you leave them wet.

DRILL OUT THE BAD PART !

How are Teeth Mended ?
Germs live in the holes of bad teeth. They eat the good part, which makes the holes deeper. Dentists have to drill out this germy part.

STOP UP THE HOLES !

The hard outside of teeth cannot grow back. Dentists have to fill the holes with metal to keep germs out.

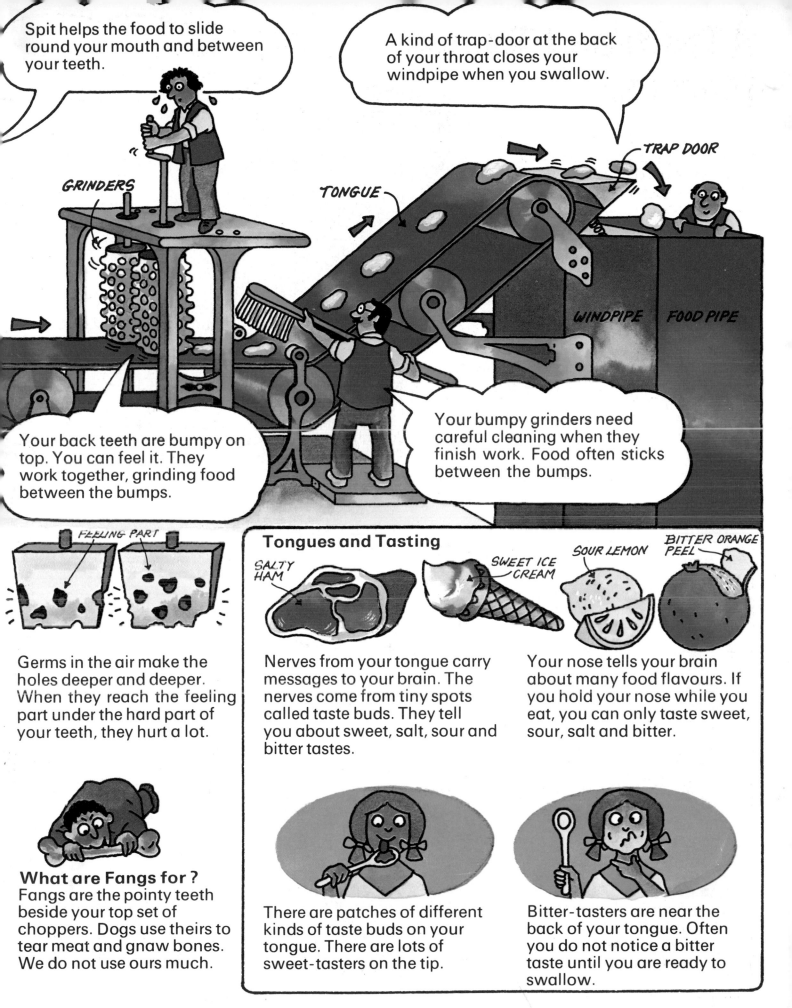

Spit helps the food to slide round your mouth and between your teeth.

A kind of trap-door at the back of your throat closes your windpipe when you swallow.

GRINDERS

TONGUE

TRAP DOOR

WINDPIPE   FOOD PIPE

Your back teeth are bumpy on top. You can feel it. They work together, grinding food between the bumps.

Your bumpy grinders need careful cleaning when they finish work. Food often sticks between the bumps.

FEELING PART

Germs in the air make the holes deeper and deeper. When they reach the feeling part under the hard part of your teeth, they hurt a lot.

What are Fangs for?
Fangs are the pointy teeth beside your top set of choppers. Dogs use theirs to tear meat and gnaw bones. We do not use ours much.

Tongues and Tasting

SALTY HAM   SWEET ICE CREAM   SOUR LEMON   BITTER ORANGE PEEL

Nerves from your tongue carry messages to your brain. The nerves come from tiny spots called taste buds. They tell you about sweet, salt, sour and bitter tastes.

Your nose tells your brain about many food flavours. If you hold your nose while you eat, you can only taste sweet, sour, salt and bitter.

There are patches of different kinds of taste buds on your tongue. There are lots of sweet-tasters on the tip.

Bitter-tasters are near the back of your tongue. Often you do not notice a bitter taste until you are ready to swallow.

What is Blood?

Most of your blood is a colourless liquid called plasma. The red cells in it make it look red.

Blood is crowded with special cells doing different kinds of work. This picture shows some of the things they do.

Your blood stream flows round your body like a river, to bring supplies to all the body cells.

HOW BLOOD GETS OXYGEN....

Red blood cells bring waste gas to your lungs. They exchange it for oxygen.

The air you breathe into your lungs carries oxygen. The air you breathe out takes away waste gas.

WATER....

Lots of water goes into your blood through the eating machinery. More than half of your blood is water.

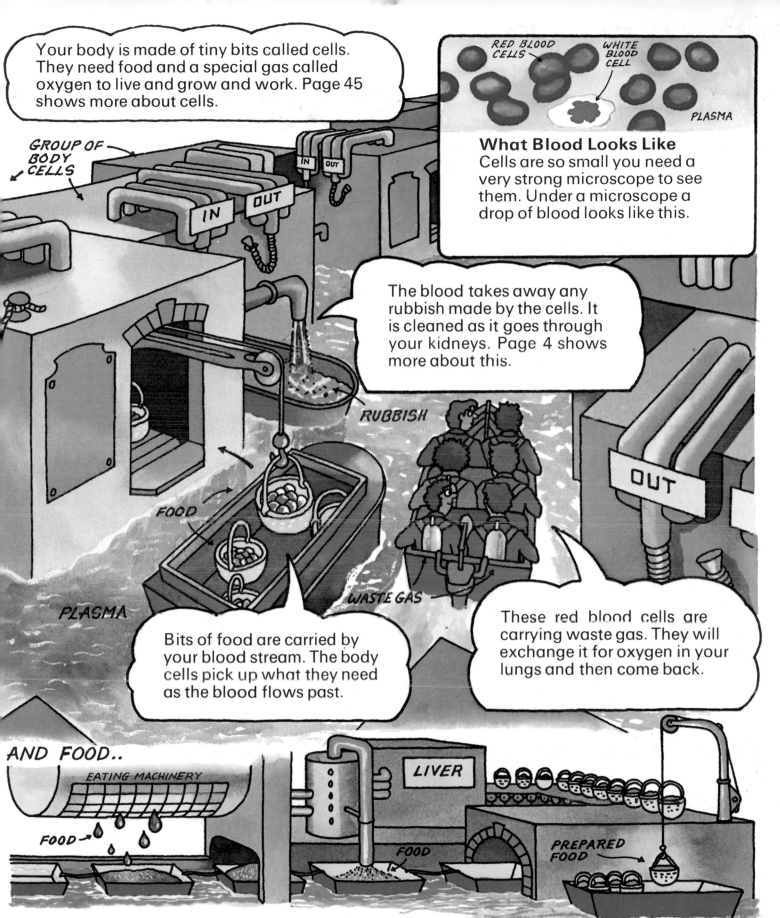

Your body is made of tiny bits called cells. They need food and a special gas called oxygen to live and grow and work. Page 45 shows more about cells.

GROUP OF BODY CELLS

IN OUT

RED BLOOD CELLS WHITE BLOOD CELL

PLASMA

What Blood Looks Like
Cells are so small you need a very strong microscope to see them. Under a microscope a drop of blood looks like this.

The blood takes away any rubbish made by the cells. It is cleaned as it goes through your kidneys. Page 4 shows more about this.

RUBBISH

OUT

FOOD

PLASMA

WASTE GAS

Bits of food are carried by your blood stream. The body cells pick up what they need as the blood flows past.

These red blood cells are carrying waste gas. They will exchange it for oxygen in your lungs and then come back.

AND FOOD..

EATING MACHINERY

FOOD

LIVER

FOOD

PREPARED FOOD

Your blood carries bits of food from your eating machinery to your liver. Your liver sorts the food.

Your liver has to change some of the food to prepare it for your body. It stores some bits. It sends other bits back into your blood.

Your blood carries food from your liver to where your body needs it.

How Blood Goes Round

Your blood stream has many tiny branches. The branches join up so that the blood goes round and round. The map at the bottom of the page shows how this happens.

Your heart is a pump that keeps blood flowing round. It squeezes out blood like a squeezy bottle. It sends blood to your lungs to get rid of waste gas and pick up oxygen. It sends blood round your body to take oxygen to all the cells.

Your blood goes through rubbery pipes called blood vessels. Page 44 shows where your main blood vessels are.

How Your Heart Works
Your heart is a muscle with four tubes, like this. The tubes are big blood vessels. The picture shows where each of them leads.

A message from the brain makes your heart squeeze. This pumps blood out and sucks it in through different tubes. Tiny gates open and shut in your heart while this happens.

BLOOD GOES TO THE LUNGS AND BACK

BLOOD GOES TO THE BODY AND BACK

Map of Big Toe

This make-believe map shows how blood vessels join up in the tip of your big toe.

The red blood river comes from your heart, bringing oxygen to body cells. The purple blood river takes away waste gas.

Notice the many tiny rivers that join the big ones. This happens all over your body.

RED BLOOD RIVER

PURPLE BLOOD RIVER

What Makes Your Heart Beat Fast?
Your body has to make lots of energy when you run or dance or play football.

Your heart has to pump very hard and fast. It has to get lots of blood up to your lungs and back to get the oxygen your body needs to make energy.

Put your hand on your chest like this when you have been running. Feel how fast your heart is beating. You breathe more quickly too.

Can Blood Run Backwards?
There are many tiny gates inside the blood vessels going to your heart. They can only move one way, like trap doors. The blood can only go up — it cannot fall back.

How to See Your Tiniest Blood Vessels
Look in the mirror. Gently pull your lower eyelid down. Under it you will see red thready bits. These are some of your tiniest blood vessels.

You have many tiny blood vessels. If you could join them all up end to end, they would stretch more than twice around the world.

How Does Your Blood Get Back to Your Heart?
As you move about, your muscles help move blood back to your heart. When you slow down your blood slows down as well.

If you wiggle your toes you can keep your feet from going to sleep. The working toe muscles speed the blood along.

Watch Your Blood Move
The blue line on the inside of your wrist is blood. Rub your thumb up it, like this. You will see the blood stop — then follow your thumb.

How You Breathe

Your lungs are full of tiny holes, like sponges. They hang in your chest, in a space made by your ribs and a special muscle. When you breathe in, your chest swells up. Air fills your lungs like water in a sponge. This machine shows how it happens.

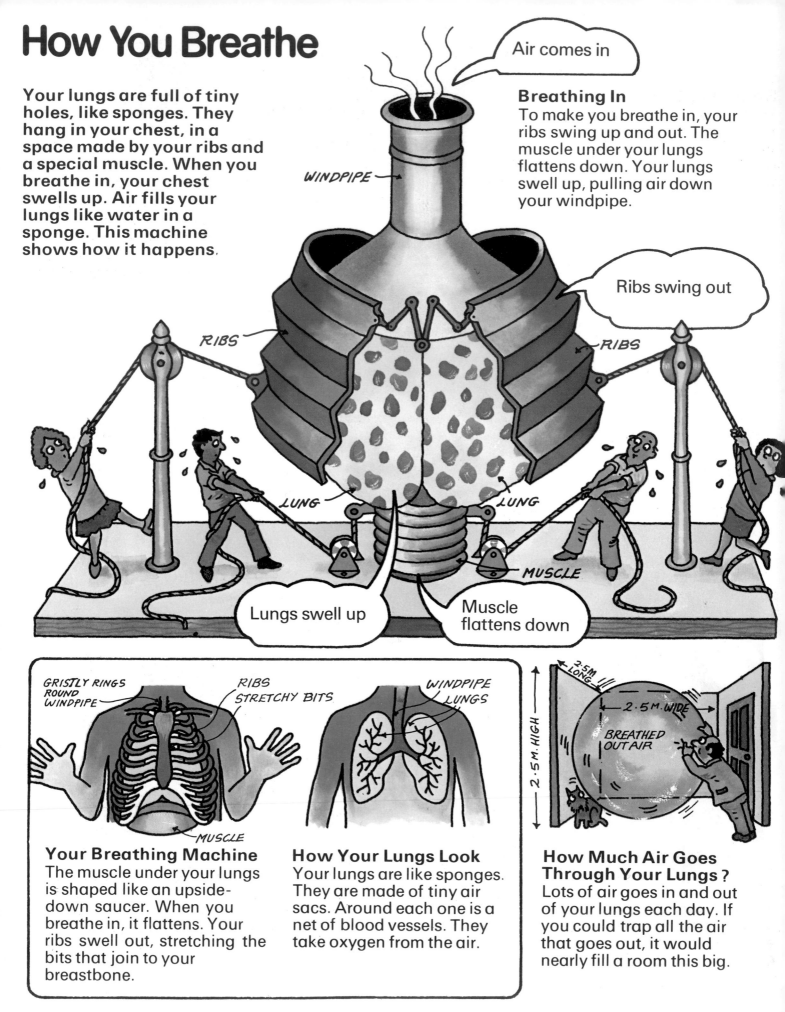

Air comes in

Breathing In
To make you breathe in, your ribs swing up and out. The muscle under your lungs flattens down. Your lungs swell up, pulling air down your windpipe.

Ribs swing out

WINDPIPE

RIBS

RIBS

LUNG

LUNG

MUSCLE

Lungs swell up

Muscle flattens down

GRISTLY RINGS ROUND WINDPIPE

RIBS STRETCHY BITS

WINDPIPE LUNGS

MUSCLE

2.5 M. LONG

2.5 M. WIDE

2.5 M. HIGH

BREATHED OUT AIR

Your Breathing Machine
The muscle under your lungs is shaped like an upside-down saucer. When you breathe in, it flattens. Your ribs swell out, stretching the bits that join to your breastbone.

How Your Lungs Look
Your lungs are like sponges. They are made of tiny air sacs. Around each one is a net of blood vessels. They take oxygen from the air.

How Much Air Goes Through Your Lungs?
Lots of air goes in and out of your lungs each day. If you could trap all the air that goes out, it would nearly fill a room this big.

Breathing Out

When you breathe out, your ribs move back. The muscle under your lungs pops up again. Air is squeezed out of the tiny air sacs in your lungs.

Feel Your Ribs Move

Cross your arms like this and take a deep breath. Feel your chest swell up? Tiny muscles criss-cross between your ribs. They make your ribs swell out.

Air goes out

WINDPIPE

Ribs fall back

RIBS

RIBS

Air is squeezed out of lungs

LUNG

LUNG

MUSCLE

Muscle pops up

Tummy Breathing

The working muscle under your lungs pushes your stomach out and in. When ladies squeezed their waists with corsets, it could not work. They often fainted.

Getting More Lung Power

If you sing or play things like trumpets, you need lots of puff. Learn to use the muscle under your lungs to get more lung power.

To practise, push the top of your stomach out as you breathe in. Hold your hand just under your chest, like this, to feel it move.

A Talking Machine

This machine does the main things that you do when you talk.

You tighten your vocal cords to make them vibrate when you breathe out. This makes sound waves — special ripples in the air. You use your teeth and tongue and mouth to turn the sound waves into words.

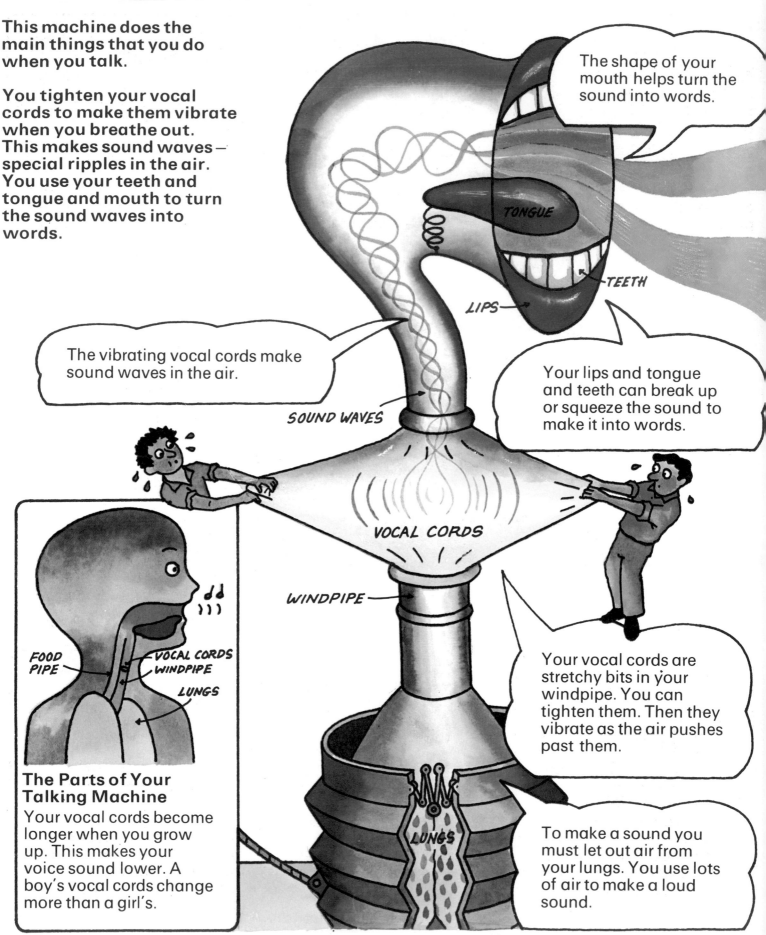

The shape of your mouth helps turn the sound into words.

TONGUE

TEETH

LIPS

The vibrating vocal cords make sound waves in the air.

SOUND WAVES

Your lips and tongue and teeth can break up or squeeze the sound to make it into words.

VOCAL CORDS

WINDPIPE

FOOD PIPE

VOCAL CORDS
WINDPIPE

LUNGS

Your vocal cords are stretchy bits in your windpipe. You can tighten them. Then they vibrate as the air pushes past them.

LUNGS

The Parts of Your Talking Machine

Your vocal cords become longer when you grow up. This makes your voice sound lower. A boy's vocal cords change more than a girl's.

To make a sound you must let out air from your lungs. You use lots of air to make a loud sound.

Making Words
The shape of your mouth changes to make different parts of words.

See how these people stretch and shape their mouths to make different sounds.

Watch yourself in the mirror while you talk. See how your own mouth changes shape.

Lip Reading
You can sometimes work out what people are saying from the shape of their mouths.

Think how useful this might be if you were a spy!

Making Sound Waves
Blow up a balloon and let it go. The rushing-out air will make the neck flap very fast. This is called vibration. Hear the sound waves it makes?

If you put a tube in the neck like this, there will be no sound as the air rushes out. The neck cannot vibrate and make sound waves.

Try stretching the neck to make high or low sounds. The wider you stretch, the lower the sound. Your vocal cords work like this.

What Ears Do

Your ear is a machine that picks up sound waves and turns them into messages to your brain. We have invented a machine that might be able to do the things your ear does. Part of it sends balance messages to your brain. Your ear does this too.

> Sound waves go through a funnel to your ear drum. They make the drum vibrate.

EAR FUNNEL

EAR DRUM

> When you blow a trumpet you make sound waves. Sound waves are like ripples in the air. You cannot see them but you can feel them.

> This funnel has wax and hairs to trap specks of dirt that might hurt the inside of your ear.

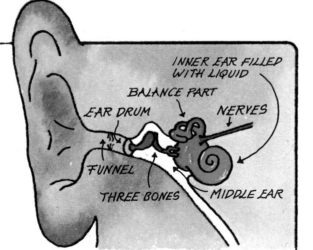

INNER EAR FILLED WITH LIQUID
BALANCE PART
EAR DRUM
NERVES
FUNNEL
THREE BONES
MIDDLE EAR

Feeling Sound Waves
Hold a cardboard tube against a balloon like this and speak into it. The sound waves will make the balloon vibrate. You can feel this with your fingers.

Your Ear Machine
Your inner ear is a curled-up tube with three extra loops. The liquid in the curled-up part picks up sound waves. The extra loops are to help you keep your balance.

What if you Only Had One Ear?
You need both ears to work out where sounds are coming from. Try this and see. Turn on the radio. Cover your eyes, cover up one ear, and turn around a few times. Where is the radio?

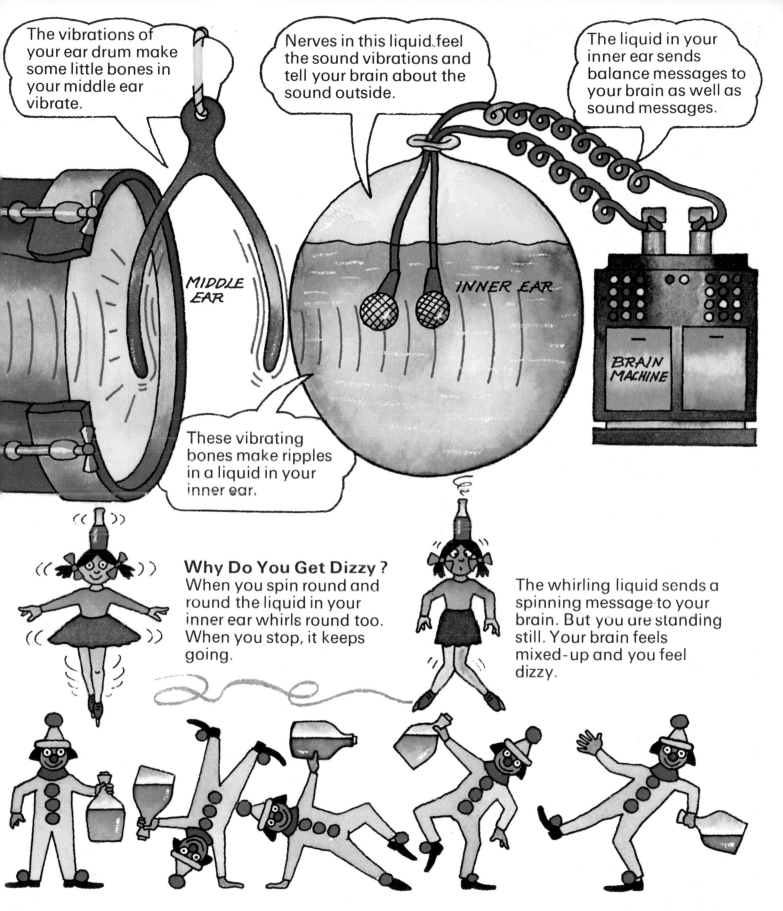

The vibrations of your ear drum make some little bones in your middle ear vibrate.

Nerves in this liquid feel the sound vibrations and tell your brain about the sound outside.

The liquid in your inner ear sends balance messages to your brain as well as sound messages.

MIDDLE EAR

INNER EAR

BRAIN MACHINE

These vibrating bones make ripples in a liquid in your inner ear.

Why Do You Get Dizzy?
When you spin round and round the liquid in your inner ear whirls round too. When you stop, it keeps going.

The whirling liquid sends a spinning message to your brain. But you are standing still. Your brain feels mixed-up and you feel dizzy.

Ears Help You Balance
The liquid in your inner ear stays level when you move, like the water in this jar.

See how the water sloshes round the jar when the jar tips and turns.

As the liquid moves around in your inner ear, nerves in the liquid tell your brain what is happening.

17

How an Eye Works

Your eye is very much like a camera. A camera takes in light rays from the outside world and squeezes them to fit on a small piece of film. Your eye gathers light rays into a very tiny picture that fits on the back of your eyeball. A nerve from this spot sends the picture to your brain.

On the right is a machine we invented to show the important parts of your eye and what they do.

Light rays from the spotlight bounce off the clown and make him see-able.

LIGHT RAYS

LIGHT RAYS

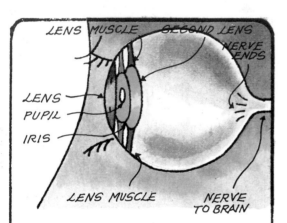

How Your Eye Looks

This picture shows where the different parts of your eye are. You can also see the muscles that change the shape of the lens inside your eye.

Light rays from the clown go through this lens. The lens bends the light rays.

What a Lens Does

A magnifying glass is a lens. You can make it bend light rays into an upside-down picture. Try this.

Hold a magnifying glass between a torch and some white paper. Move the glass backwards and forwards until you see a clear pattern of light on the paper. You may have to move the paper.

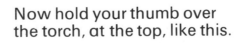

Now hold your thumb over the torch, at the top, like this.

Where is your thumb in the pattern on the paper?

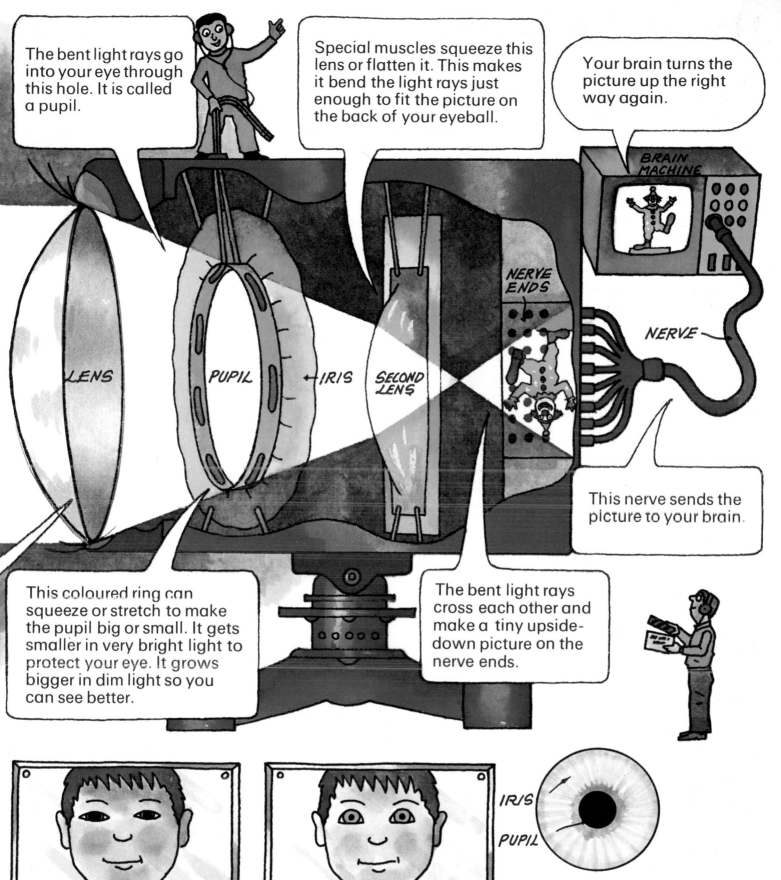

The bent light rays go into your eye through this hole. It is called a pupil.

Special muscles squeeze this lens or flatten it. This makes it bend the light rays just enough to fit the picture on the back of your eyeball.

Your brain turns the picture up the right way again.

BRAIN MACHINE

NERVE ENDS

NERVE

LENS

PUPIL

←IRIS

SECOND LENS

This nerve sends the picture to your brain.

This coloured ring can squeeze or stretch to make the pupil big or small. It gets smaller in very bright light to protect your eye. It grows bigger in dim light so you can see better.

The bent light rays cross each other and make a tiny upside-down picture on the nerve ends.

IRIS

PUPIL

How Your Pupil Shrinks
The coloured ring round your pupil is called the iris. If you look closely, you can see rays. These are muscles that pull your iris in and out.

Watch Your Pupil Shrink
Look in the mirror. Close your eyes nearly shut. Your pupils will get bigger.

Now open your eyes quickly. Watch carefully and you will see your pupils shrinking.

How Two Eyes Work Together

Each of your eyes sees a slightly different picture of the world. Your brain puts the two pictures together. On this page you can see how the picture changes in your brain.

When you look at something very close, it is easy to notice the difference in what your two eyes see. Just try this trick:

See-Through Pencil Trick
Print a word in large letters on some paper. Hold a pencil half-way between your eyes and the paper. If you close either eye, part of the word will be hidden. But if you stare hard at the paper with both eyes, you will see the whole word.

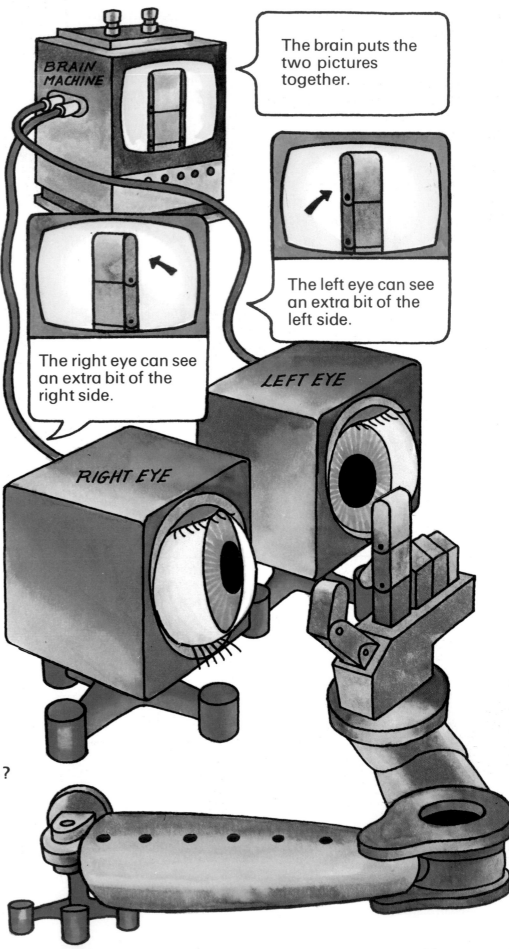

The brain puts the two pictures together.

The left eye can see an extra bit of the left side.

The right eye can see an extra bit of the right side.

Why Do You Have Two Eyes?
Close one eye. Hold a pencil in one hand. Stretch out your arm like this and try to touch something. Can you do it? Two eyes working together help you to see how close things are.

What Noses Do

This picture shows how your nose cleans and warms the air you breathe. The air is full of germs and tiny specks of dirt. We have made them into bugs so you can see how they get trapped.

A special gas floats away from things that have a smell. We have made it look like stars to show what happens to it.

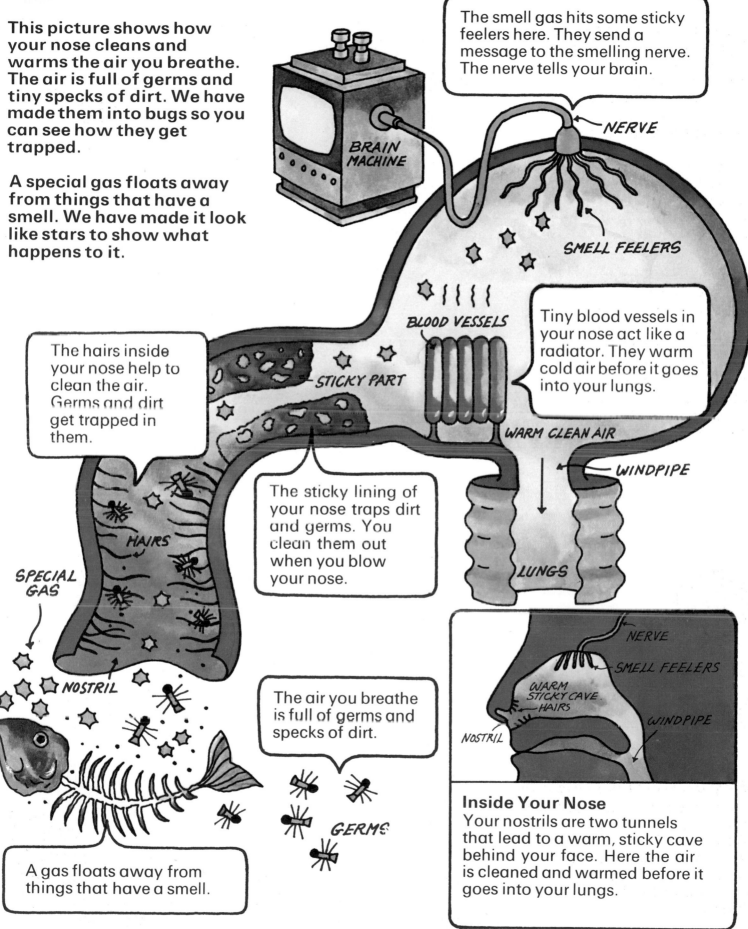

The smell gas hits some sticky feelers here. They send a message to the smelling nerve. The nerve tells your brain.

NERVE

SMELL FEELERS

BRAIN MACHINE

BLOOD VESSELS

Tiny blood vessels in your nose act like a radiator. They warm cold air before it goes into your lungs.

STICKY PART

WARM CLEAN AIR

WINDPIPE

The hairs inside your nose help to clean the air. Germs and dirt get trapped in them.

HAIRS

SPECIAL GAS

NOSTRIL

The sticky lining of your nose traps dirt and germs. You clean them out when you blow your nose.

LUNGS

The air you breathe is full of germs and specks of dirt.

GERMS

A gas floats away from things that have a smell.

NERVE

SMELL FEELERS

WARM STICKY CAVE

HAIRS

WINDPIPE

NOSTRIL

Inside Your Nose
Your nostrils are two tunnels that lead to a warm, sticky cave behind your face. Here the air is cleaned and warmed before it goes into your lungs.

A Feeling Machine

Tiny nerves in your skin tell you if things are hot or cold, hard or soft, rough or smooth. Your fingers have many nerves. You use them a lot for finding out about things.

This machine explores the world, like your fingers. Its feelers act like the nerves in your skin. Each kind of feeler tests for something special.

The brain gets messages from all these feelers.

This feeler tests for coldness.

These feelers test for smoothness or roughness. They pick up light and gentle touches.

This feeler tests the heat of things.

This pressure feeler sends messages about bumps. It presses things to test for hardness.

Any feeling that is too strong — like a hard bump or too much heat — becomes a pain message. It tells your brain that something is hurting you.

Touching, Feeling, Finding Out

Your brain gets feeling messages from nerves in your skin and nerves all through your body. These messages fool your brain sometimes. Read on and see why this happens.

The next pages show how your brain sorts out messages from your body.

Mysterious Pains
Tiny hurts on places like your feet and tongue can feel enormous. Why?

These places are crowded with feeling nerves. Your brain gets lots of pain messages — but they all come from one tiny spot.

Feely Box Trick
For this trick you need a box with two hand-holes and some things that feel funny.

Put the things inside, one by one, through your side. Get your friends to stick their hands through the other hole and guess what is inside.

Itchy Back Problems
The nerves on your back are far apart. A big space may have only one nerve. It is hard to tell just where a tickle itches.

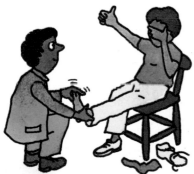

Your Muscle Nerves
If someone wiggles your toe, you can tell without looking whether the toe is up or down. You get messages from feeling nerves in your muscles.

Why Do You Have Pains?
Nerves inside your body tell you when something is hurting your inside. This helps people to know what to do when you are ill.

Back Feeler Trick
Touch someone's back with a pencil. Then touch with two pencils at the same time. If the two pencils are closer than 2 cm, he may still think there is only one.

What Happens in Your Brain

Your brain is a bit like a busy telephone system that receives and sends out lots of messages.
We made up this machine to show how the messages go through the main parts of your brain.

Here are Your Five Senses
Your senses bring messages about the world.
Your memory helps to work out what they mean.

HEARING
YOUR EARS HEAR THIS NOISE—
YOUR MEMORY SAYS—
"CAR!"

SIGHT
YOUR EYES SEE THIS!

YOUR MEMORY SAYS—
"WATCH OUT!"

SMELL
YOUR NOSE SMELLS THIS—
YOUR MEMORY SAYS—"IT MIGHT BE CAKE!"

TASTE
YOUR TONGUE SAYS SOUR! YOUR MEMORY SAYS "NOT RIPE!"

KEEP OUT

TOUCH
THE SKIN OF YOUR FINGERS FEELS BUMPS AND HAIR. YOUR MEMORY HELPS YOU WORK OUT WHO IT IS.

This part gets important news from your senses. This helps it work out plans for action. It can shut out some messages that are not important.

HEARING
SIGHT
SMELL
TASTE
TOUCH

MESSAGE ROOM

This part gets lots of messages from your senses. It checks with your memory to help work out what they mean.

DIGESTION

HEARTBEAT

Nerves carry messages from your senses to your brain.

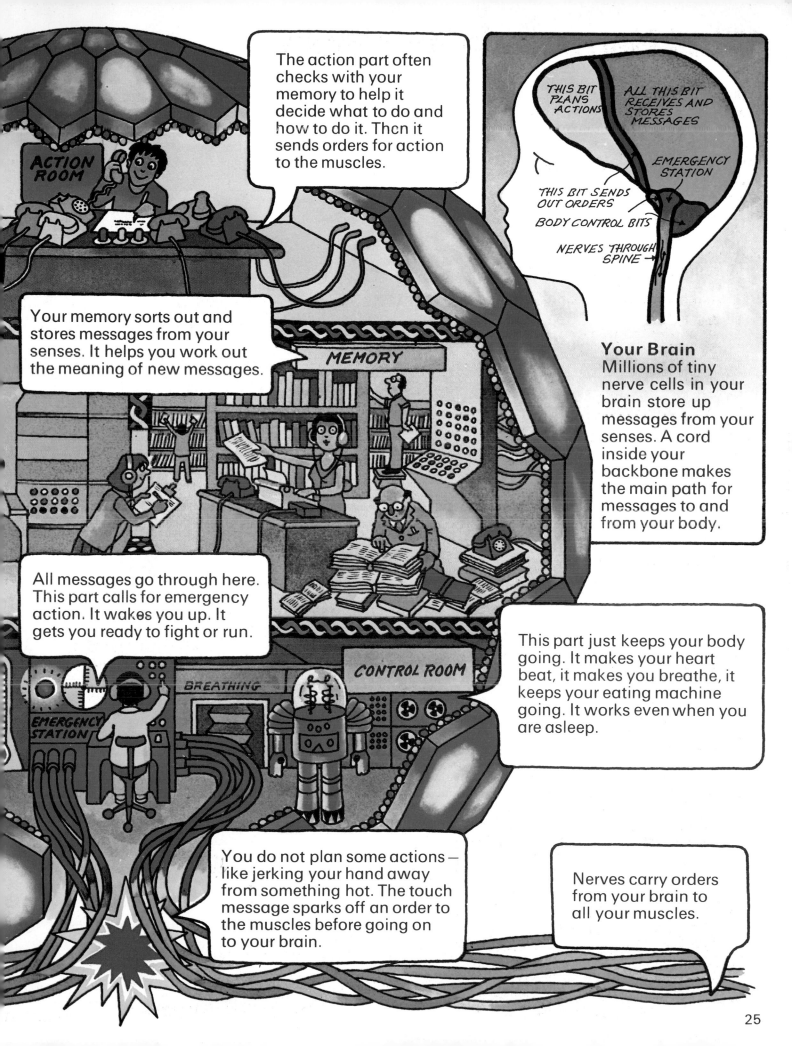

The action part often checks with your memory to help it decide what to do and how to do it. Then it sends orders for action to the muscles.

THIS BIT PLANS ACTIONS

ALL THIS BIT RECEIVES AND STORES MESSAGES

EMERGENCY STATION

THIS BIT SENDS OUT ORDERS

BODY CONTROL BITS

NERVES THROUGH SPINE

ACTION ROOM

Your memory sorts out and stores messages from your senses. It helps you work out the meaning of new messages.

MEMORY

Your Brain
Millions of tiny nerve cells in your brain store up messages from your senses. A cord inside your backbone makes the main path for messages to and from your body.

All messages go through here. This part calls for emergency action. It wakes you up. It gets you ready to fight or run.

EMERGENCY STATION

BREATHING

CONTROL ROOM

This part just keeps your body going. It makes your heart beat, it makes you breathe, it keeps your eating machine going. It works even when you are asleep.

You do not plan some actions — like jerking your hand away from something hot. The touch message sparks off an order to the muscles before going on to your brain.

Nerves carry orders from your brain to all your muscles.

Alarm...

You are sleeping soundly in a quiet room. Suddenly there is a scuffle at the open window.

You open your eyes and see a strange, dark shape. At first, you are terrified. You reach out and turn on the lamp.

Most of the brain is resting but the control room is always busy. And the emergency station is always ready for action. Just watch it now.

Now the newsroom can find out more about the strange noise. The action part can get the body's muscles going.

A Story of Your Brain in Action

Oh, it's only the owl that lives in the tree outside. He gives a hoot, to prove it, before he flies away.

You turn off the light and go to sleep again.

Here the brain is using messages from many senses to work out what is happening. It uses memories, too.

The emergency is over. Most of the brain shuts down. The emergency station will take over now, to watch over the body while it sleeps.

Your earflap is made of gristle, not bone. It is bendy, like the end of your nose.

Your brain is protected by a helmet of bone. Your eyes look out from holes in it.

Your head sits on your backbone, like a ring on a peg. This lets you nod and turn and roll it.

A ball rolls in a socket when you circle your arm. Your hip works like this, too.

Run your fingers down your backbone. The spaces between bumps are joints. The bumps move apart when you bend forward.

Your thumb joint can move in special ways to let you hold things between your fingers and thumb.

The joints of your fingers and toes are a bit like door hinges.

How Bones Fit Together

The places where your bones link up are called joints. This made-up skeleton shows how your main joints work.

This skeleton will not work as well as yours. Its metal pieces will be hard to move. Real bone is light. It is full of tiny holes, like honeycomb.

Many little joints in your feet and ankles move when you run. Try to run on your heels and see the difference.

This is Your Skeleton
Muscles join these sticking-out bits. Pads of gristle make cushions between each two bones.

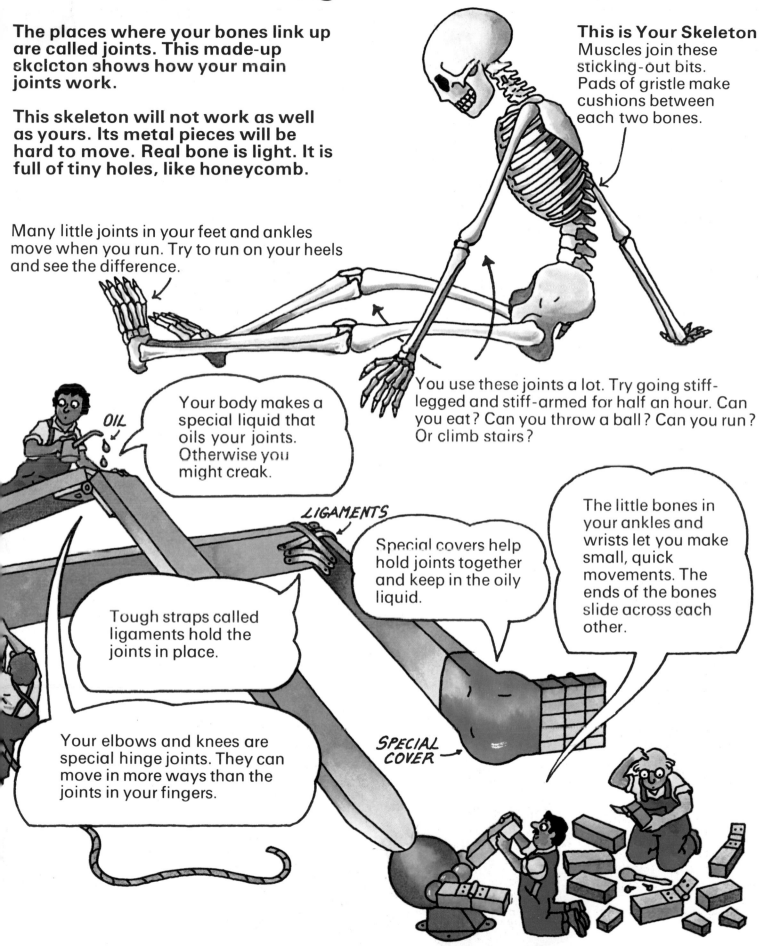

You use these joints a lot. Try going stiff-legged and stiff-armed for half an hour. Can you eat? Can you throw a ball? Can you run? Or climb stairs?

OIL

Your body makes a special liquid that oils your joints. Otherwise you might creak.

LIGAMENTS

Special covers help hold joints together and keep in the oily liquid.

The little bones in your ankles and wrists let you make small, quick movements. The ends of the bones slide across each other.

Tough straps called ligaments hold the joints in place.

SPECIAL COVER

Your elbows and knees are special hinge joints. They can move in more ways than the joints in your fingers.

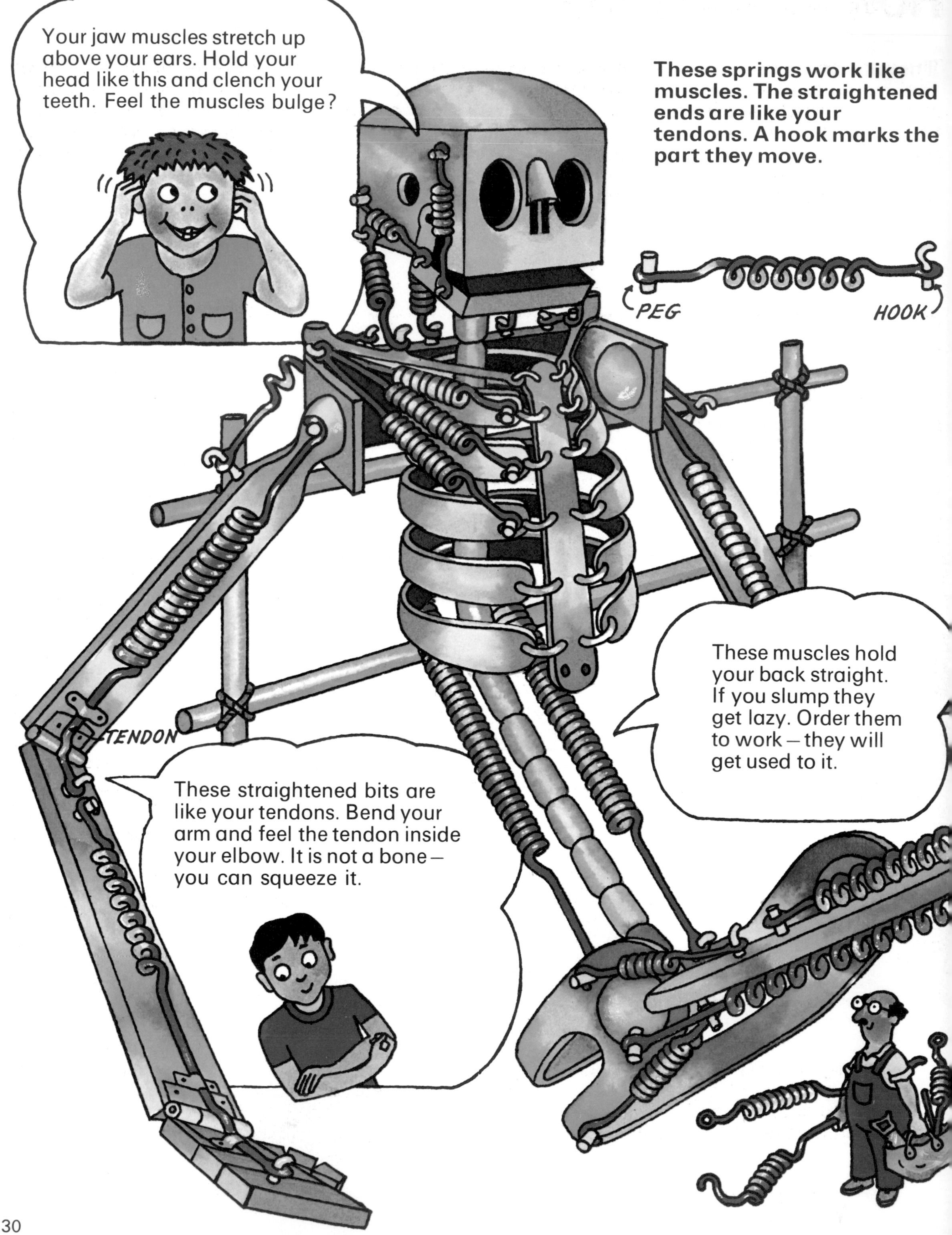

Your jaw muscles stretch up above your ears. Hold your head like this and clench your teeth. Feel the muscles bulge?

These springs work like muscles. The straightened ends are like your tendons. A hook marks the part they move.

PEG

HOOK

These muscles hold your back straight. If you slump they get lazy. Order them to work — they will get used to it.

TENDON

These straightened bits are like your tendons. Bend your arm and feel the tendon inside your elbow. It is not a bone — you can squeeze it.

How Muscles Work

The springs on this skeleton work like muscles. Look to see how they join the movable parts. They work these bits the way your muscles work your bones.

Nerves connect these muscles to your brain. Messages from your brain make them work. Your brain can send many messages and work many muscles at the same time.

Other muscles work things inside you, like your heart and eating machinery. A special part of your brain keeps these muscles going.

Muscles Work in Pairs

Each joint is worked by two muscles. They work in turn, like this. Hold your arm near your elbow and waggle your wrist. You can feel these muscles bulge in turn.

1

2

Look for the bulge when you waggle your foot. The working muscle is up near your knee.

A Pair of Your Muscles Looks a Bit Like This

MUSCLES

This big tendon carries the whole weight of your body. Feel how hard it is when you stand on one foot, like this.

Leg muscles keep you upright, like the muscles in your neck and back. Most of the time you hardly notice they are working.

BIG LEG TENDON

What Skin Does

All over your body is a coat of skin. You can only see the surface of it. On this page we have made a huge picture of a piece of skin to show what happens underneath.

The skin you see is a layer of dead bits. This layer is dry and tough and waterproof. It protects your body from germs and from drying up.

Just under it is a second layer where new skin is made. These bits are fed by blood vessels in the deep layer. They die as they get pushed up to the surface.

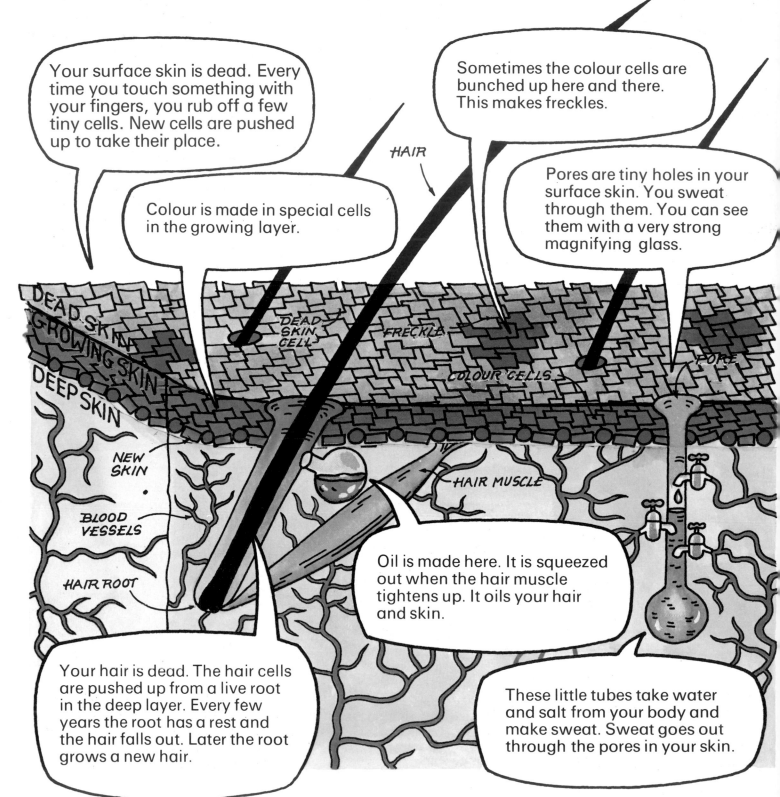

Your surface skin is dead. Every time you touch something with your fingers, you rub off a few tiny cells. New cells are pushed up to take their place.

Colour is made in special cells in the growing layer.

HAIR

Sometimes the colour cells are bunched up here and there. This makes freckles.

Pores are tiny holes in your surface skin. You sweat through them. You can see them with a very strong magnifying glass.

DEAD SKIN
GROWING SKIN
DEEP SKIN

DEAD SKIN CELL
FRECKLE
COLOUR CELLS
PORE

NEW SKIN

BLOOD VESSELS

HAIR ROOT

HAIR MUSCLE

Oil is made here. It is squeezed out when the hair muscle tightens up. It oils your hair and skin.

Your hair is dead. The hair cells are pushed up from a live root in the deep layer. Every few years the root has a rest and the hair falls out. Later the root grows a new hair.

These little tubes take water and salt from your body and make sweat. Sweat goes out through the pores in your skin.

What Would Happen If You Had No Skin?

Your body is made mostly of water. There is even some water in your bones. If you had no skin, the sun and air would dry you up like a prune.

Skin is Waterproof

Your skin makes oil which helps to keep it waterproof. Water does not soak into your skin. You can rub it off with a towel.

Why Should You Wash?

Dirt and dust from the air stick to the oil made by your skin. You have to use soap and warm water to get the dirty oil off.

When it is Hot and Sunny

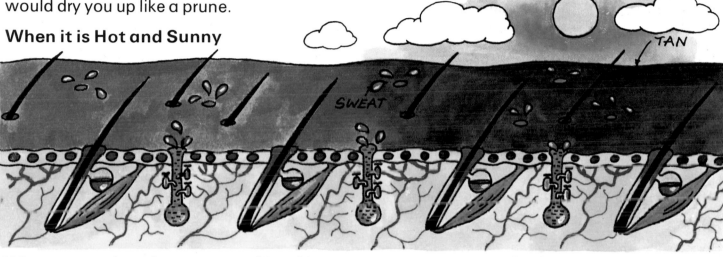

When you are hot, the sweat glands make more sweat. The sweat goes out through pores in your skin. As it dries, it cools down your skin.

Your blood takes heat from your body. When you are hot, more blood moves through the vessels near the surface of your skin. Then the air can cool it.

Sunlight makes the colour cells go darker. Some of the sun's rays are bad for you. Dark skin protects your body from the harmful rays.

When it is Cold

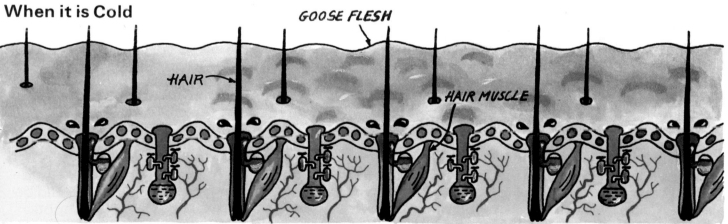

The air takes heat from your skin. When it is cold your blood vessels squeeze down in your skin to keep the warmth in. This makes you look paler.

Cold makes your hair muscles tighten. Then your hair stands up. On furry animals, hair traps a blanket of warm air. This helps to keep them warm.

When a hair muscle tightens, it gets short and fat. This squeezes out oil, makes your hair stand up, and makes goose flesh on your skin.

How Bodies Fight Germs

Your body is always being attacked by germs. But it is well defended, like the castle in this picture. Your skin is a strong wall – like a castle wall.

Germs cannot get through healthy skin. If skin is hurt, cells in the blood help to heal it and fight off the germs. They act like the warriors here.

Germs can get into your body through openings like your mouth and nose. But each of these is protected in some way. And there are ways you can help your body to defend itself. Look round and see.

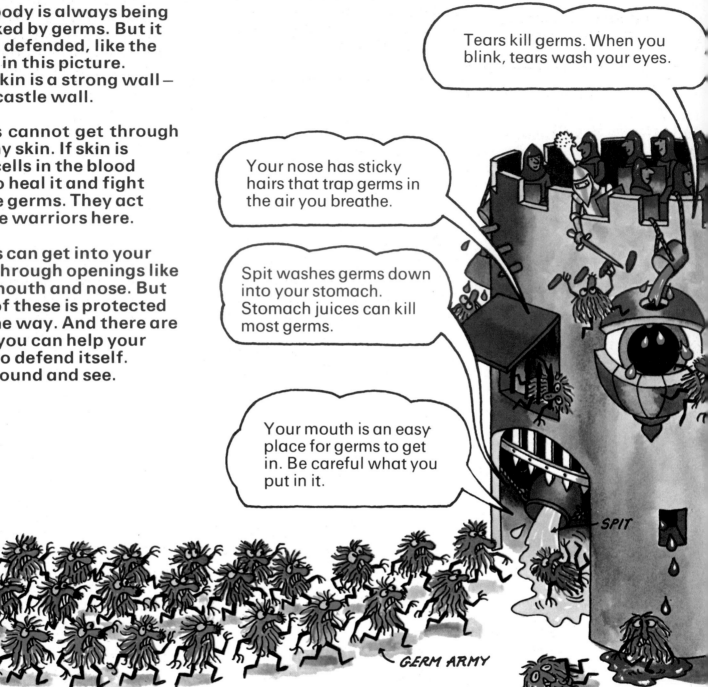

Tears kill germs. When you blink, tears wash your eyes.

Your nose has sticky hairs that trap germs in the air you breathe.

Spit washes germs down into your stomach. Stomach juices can kill most germs.

Your mouth is an easy place for germs to get in. Be careful what you put in it.

SPIT

GERM ARMY

What are Germs?
Germs are tiny creatures, too small to see. If they get into your body they make you ill. They make poisons. They become powerful armies.

Germs like warm, dark, dirty places. Sun and fresh air kill them. Soapy water kills them. Good food helps your body make weapons to fight them.

Why do You Get Injections?
Some germs have secret weapons. If a lot of them made a surprise attack you would be very ill. So the Doctor shoots some weak germs into you.

NEEDLE

34

The illustration is a castle-defence metaphor for the body's defences, with the following speech bubbles and labels:

> Your ear hole has wax and hairs to trap germs.

> Special white cells in your blood fight germs. Different kinds do different jobs. Some of them corner the germs and others kill them.

> Your blood is always moving round your body. When germs attack, your blood carries messages for help. Then lots of fighting white cells come.

> Repair cells make a net and other cells bunch up behind it. Then blood cannot run out and germs cannot get in.

> Your blood has special repair cells. When you are cut they make some gluey stuff that turns tiny bits in your blood into a net.

> Tiny holes called pores let out sweat. Clean sweat kills germs. But old sweat traps dirt — so wash it off.

Labels in the illustration: RED BLOOD CELLS, WHITE BLOOD CELL, EAR HOLE, CUT →, SWEAT PORES

Your blood cells learn about the new weapons from the weak germs, and work out how to destroy them. Then you are prepared for an attack.

What is a Scab?

Part of your blood makes a net when you are cut. Your blood cells bunch up behind it. This makes a blood clot. Dried clotted blood becomes a scab.

The scab protects you while new skin is built. When the new skin is ready, the scab falls off.

Shopping-Trip Game

On the right are pictures of seven important kinds of food. You need a little of each kind at least every few days to stay really fit and healthy.

Play this game to practice choosing the right kinds of food.

The object of this game is to get some of each of the seven important kinds of food before you get Home. Make a score card like the one shown below. Mark it each time you land on a food square. The winner is the first player Home with a Seven-Up.

Sweets take up room needed for important things. If you score more than one of these, you must return to Start.

Rules
Each player needs a counter, a pencil and a score card. Throw a dice to see how many places you may move. Score your card every time you land on a food square. If you collect two sweet things cross out both and return to Start. If you get Home without a Seven-Up, return to Start. You may use your turn to swap places with another player. He does not lose his next turn.

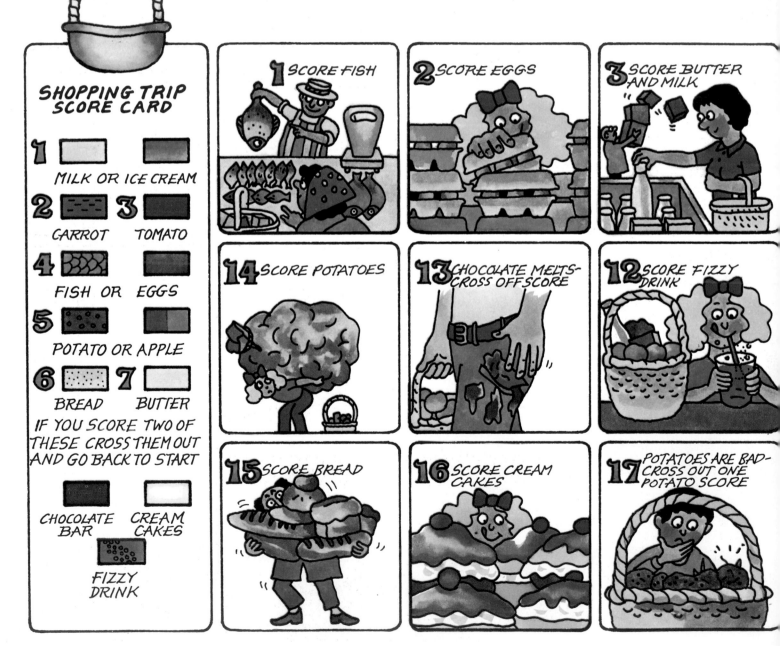

SHOPPING TRIP SCORE CARD

1 — MILK OR ICE CREAM

2 CARROT   3 TOMATO

4 FISH OR   EGGS

5 POTATO OR APPLE

6 BREAD   7 BUTTER

IF YOU SCORE TWO OF THESE CROSS THEM OUT AND GO BACK TO START

CHOCOLATE BAR   CREAM CAKES

FIZZY DRINK

1 SCORE FISH

2 SCORE EGGS

3 SCORE BUTTER AND MILK

14 SCORE POTATOES

13 CHOCOLATE MELTS- CROSS OFF SCORE

12 SCORE FIZZY DRINK

15 SCORE BREAD

16 SCORE CREAM CAKES

17 POTATOES ARE BAD- CROSS OUT ONE POTATO SCORE

Food Groups

1 Milk and cheese for strong bones and healthy teeth.

2 Leafy green and yellow vegetables for shiny hair and good skin.

3 These help to fight germs — especially cold germs.

4 Meat, fish and eggs for good muscle.

5 Brown bread and cereals for energy.

6 These vegetables and fruit help all round.

7 Butter for healthy skin and hair.

4 SCORE ICE CREAM

5 EGGS BROKEN. CROSS OUT ONE EGG SCORE.

6 ICE CREAM MELTS — CROSS OUT SCORE.

7 SCORE CHOCOLATE BAR

11 FISH LOST — CROSS OUT ONE FISH SCORE

10 SCORE TOMATOES

9 SCORE APPLES

8 SCORE CARROTS

18 DROP CREAM CAKES — CROSS OFF SCORE

19 APPLE HAS WORM CROSS OUT ONE APPLE SCORE

20 TOMATOES SQUASHED CROSS OUT ONE TOMATO SCORE

HOME

How a Baby Starts

A baby starts when two special cells meet — a sperm cell from a man's body and an egg cell from a woman's body. Joined inside the woman's body, these two cells grow into a whole new person.

Men and women each have special bits for making these cells and helping them join up. We made up these Mum and Dad machines to show how they work.

The Dad Machine

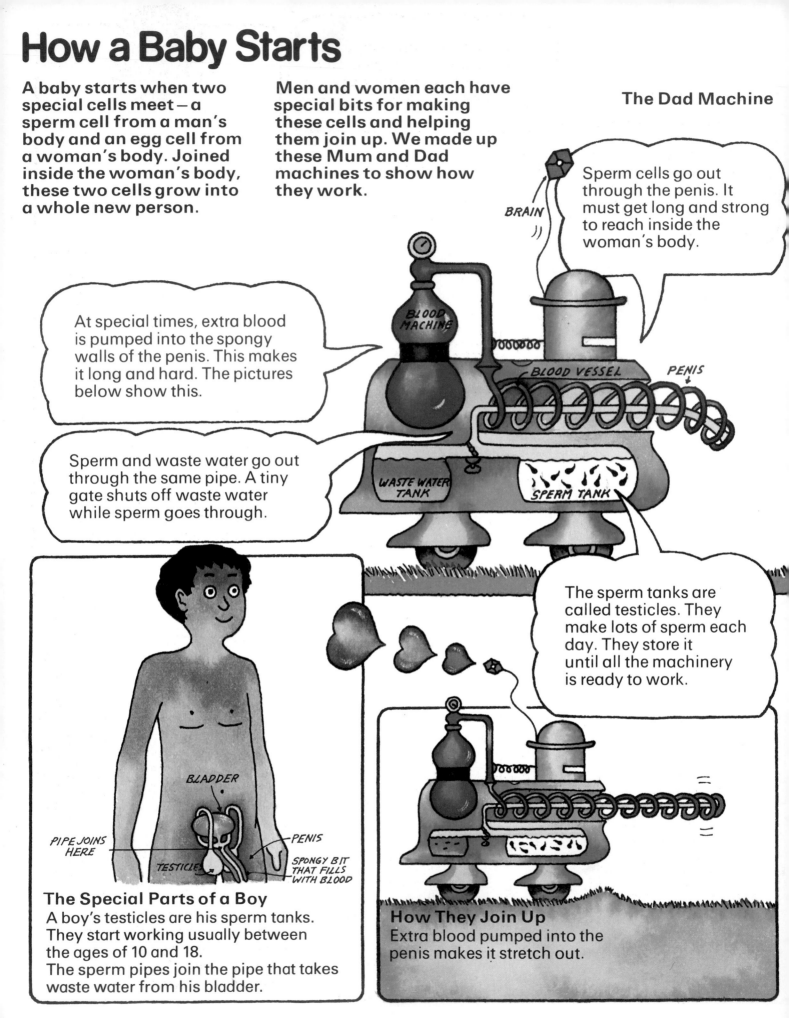

Sperm cells go out through the penis. It must get long and strong to reach inside the woman's body.

BRAIN

At special times, extra blood is pumped into the spongy walls of the penis. This makes it long and hard. The pictures below show this.

BLOOD MACHINE

BLOOD VESSEL

PENIS

Sperm and waste water go out through the same pipe. A tiny gate shuts off waste water while sperm goes through.

WASTE WATER TANK

SPERM TANK

The sperm tanks are called testicles. They make lots of sperm each day. They store it until all the machinery is ready to work.

BLADDER

PIPE JOINS HERE

PENIS

TESTICLES

SPONGY BIT THAT FILLS WITH BLOOD

The Special Parts of a Boy

A boy's testicles are his sperm tanks. They start working usually between the ages of 10 and 18.
The sperm pipes join the pipe that takes waste water from his bladder.

How They Join Up

Extra blood pumped into the penis makes it stretch out.

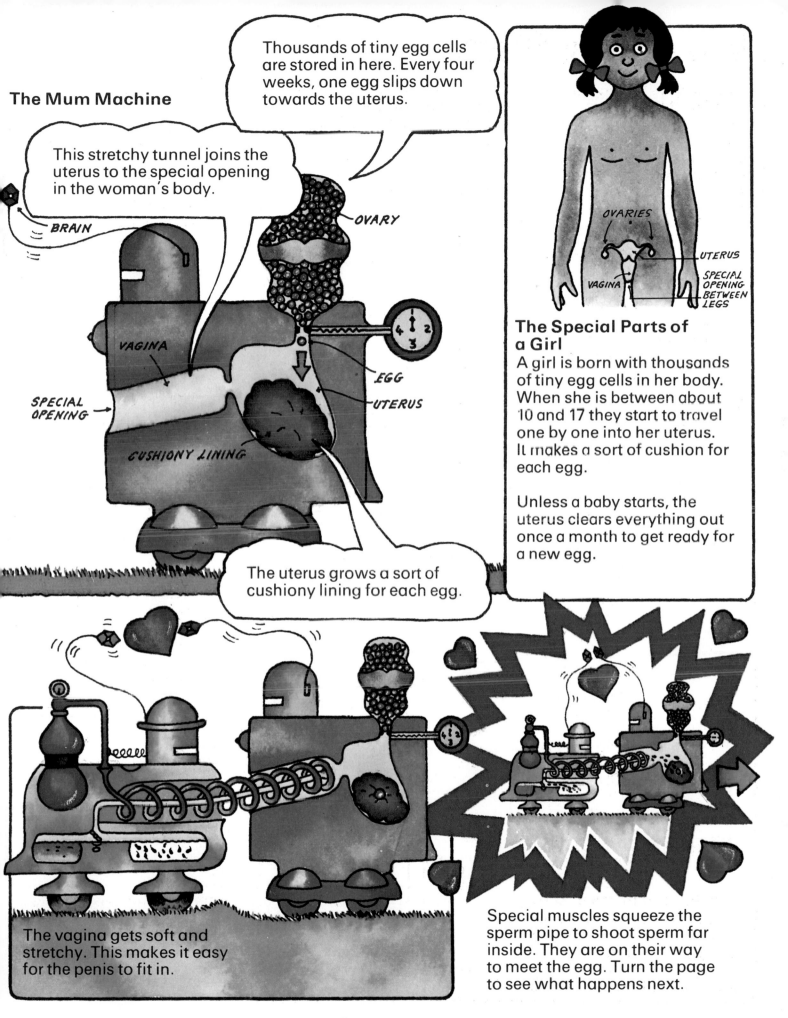

The Mum Machine

Thousands of tiny egg cells are stored in here. Every four weeks, one egg slips down towards the uterus.

This stretchy tunnel joins the uterus to the special opening in the woman's body.

BRAIN

OVARY

VAGINA

SPECIAL OPENING

CUSHIONY LINING

EGG

UTERUS

The uterus grows a sort of cushiony lining for each egg.

OVARIES

UTERUS

VAGINA

SPECIAL OPENING BETWEEN LEGS

The Special Parts of a Girl

A girl is born with thousands of tiny egg cells in her body. When she is between about 10 and 17 they start to travel one by one into her uterus. It makes a sort of cushion for each egg.

Unless a baby starts, the uterus clears everything out once a month to get ready for a new egg.

The vagina gets soft and stretchy. This makes it easy for the penis to fit in.

Special muscles squeeze the sperm pipe to shoot sperm far inside. They are on their way to meet the egg. Turn the page to see what happens next.

How a Baby is Born

These pictures show the main things that happen as a baby grows in its mother and as it is born.

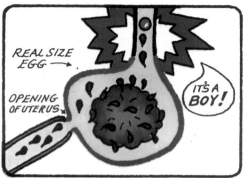

No one knows yet that a baby has started.

The Mum's Story

The baby is just a dot inside the mum.

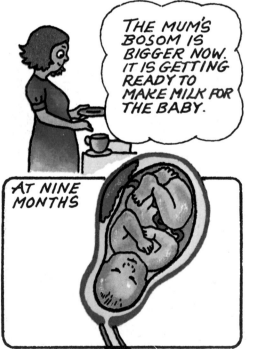

The Baby's Story
First, sperms swim up to meet the egg. A sperm is much smaller than an egg. It has the message that decides whether a boy or girl is made.

Real size egg →
Opening of uterus
It's a boy!

At the beginning...
The egg is joined by just one sperm. It grows by splitting into more cells which quickly grow and split again. The growing egg nestles down into the lining of the uterus.

At one month...
The cluster of cells is about the size of a small bean. It has grown a water bag around itself. The growing baby floats inside, warm and safe.

Water bag

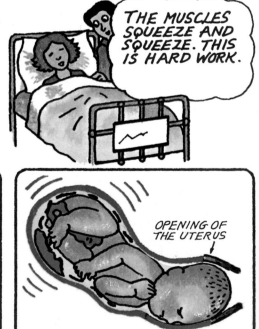

The mum's bosom is bigger now. It is getting ready to make milk for the baby.

When the muscles squeeze, she knows the baby will soon be born.

The muscles squeeze and squeeze. This is hard work.

At nine months
The baby is ready to be born now. His head is down, like this. This will help when the muscles of the uterus start to push him out.

At the start of a birth
The muscles of the uterus begin to squeeze and stretch, to make the opening wide. The baby's water bag bursts — he does not need it any more.

The muscles have worked for hours now. See how wide the opening of the uterus is. The baby's head is pressing against it — this helps.

Opening of the uterus

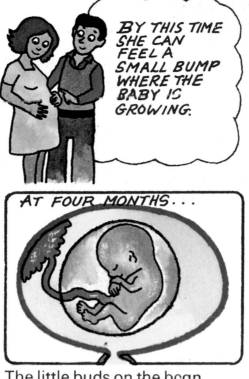

NOW THE MUM KNOWS A BABY HAS STARTED – HER UTERUS HAS KEPT ITS SPECIAL LINING.

BY THIS TIME SHE CAN FEEL A SMALL BUMP WHERE THE BABY IS GROWING.

SOMETIMES SHE CAN FEEL THE BABY KICK!

AT TWO MONTHS...

FEEDING STEM

Now the baby looks a bit like this. It grows on a sort of stem. Food and oxygen from the blood in the lining of the uterus go through the stem to the baby.

AT FOUR MONTHS...

The little buds on the bean shape have grown into arms and legs now. The cluster of cells is a complete baby. But he is still too weak to live in the outside world.

AT FIVE MONTHS...

The baby grows bigger and stronger every day. He can move about now – he even kicks sometimes. The doctor can hear his heart beating.

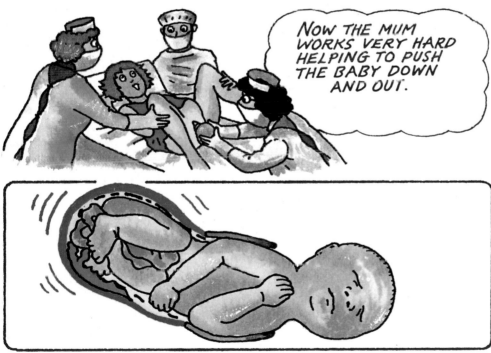

NOW THE MUM WORKS VERY HARD HELPING TO PUSH THE BABY DOWN AND OUT.

Now the muscles of the uterus begin to squeeze very hard. They push the baby's head right through the opening of the uterus.

Then the baby slides through the mother's vagina. This little tunnel can stretch very wide for the baby to go through.

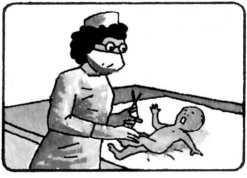

And the baby is born. His feeding stem is snipped and tied – his own lungs and eating machinery will do that work now. The knot becomes a tummy button, just like yours.

How Your Body Fits Together~1

These pictures show some of the main parts of your body. Trace the skeleton to see how your bones fit your breathing and eating machinery.

Pictures on the next pages show your main nerves and blood vessels. The skeleton fits these pictures too.

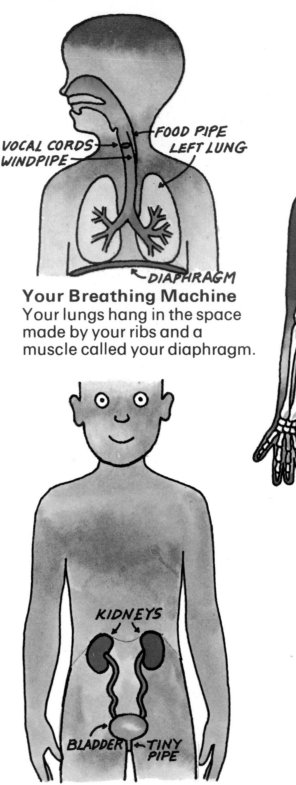

Your Breathing Machine
Your lungs hang in the space made by your ribs and a muscle called your diaphragm.

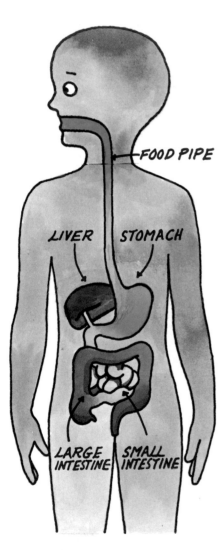

Your Eating Machine
Fine thready bits hold your intestines to your backbone. Stomach and back muscles help protect them.

How Waste Water Goes Out
Waste water stored in your bladder goes out through a tiny pipe. A boy's pipe is longer than a girl's.

Your Skeleton
There are more than 200 bones in your skeleton.

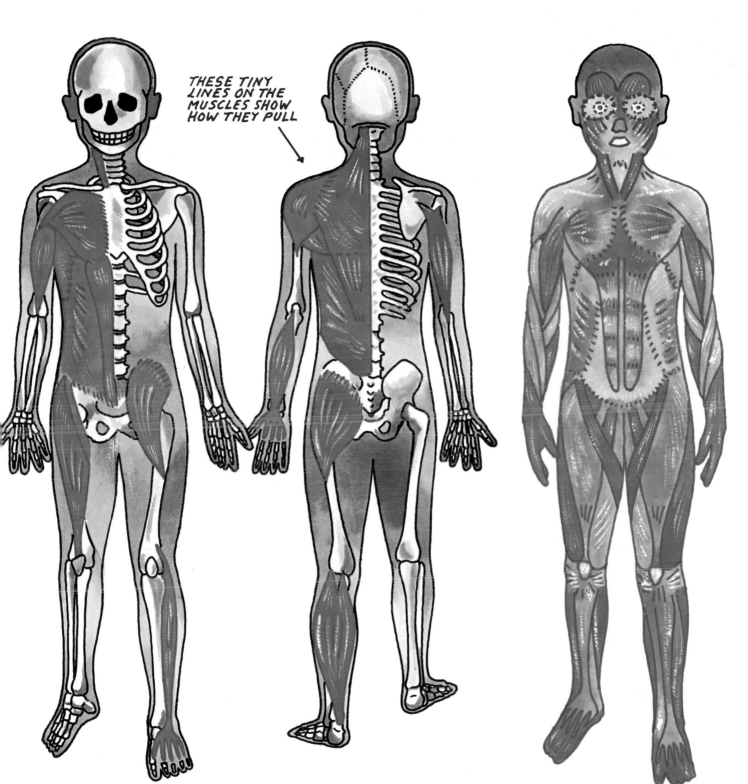

THESE TINY LINES ON THE MUSCLES SHOW HOW THEY PULL

Important Front Muscles
These are some of the main muscles that join the front of your skeleton.

Important Back Muscles
This picture shows some of the big muscles that join the back of your skeleton.

How Muscles Look
Hundreds of muscles weave together like this to make the fleshy cover of your body.

How Your Body Fits Together~2

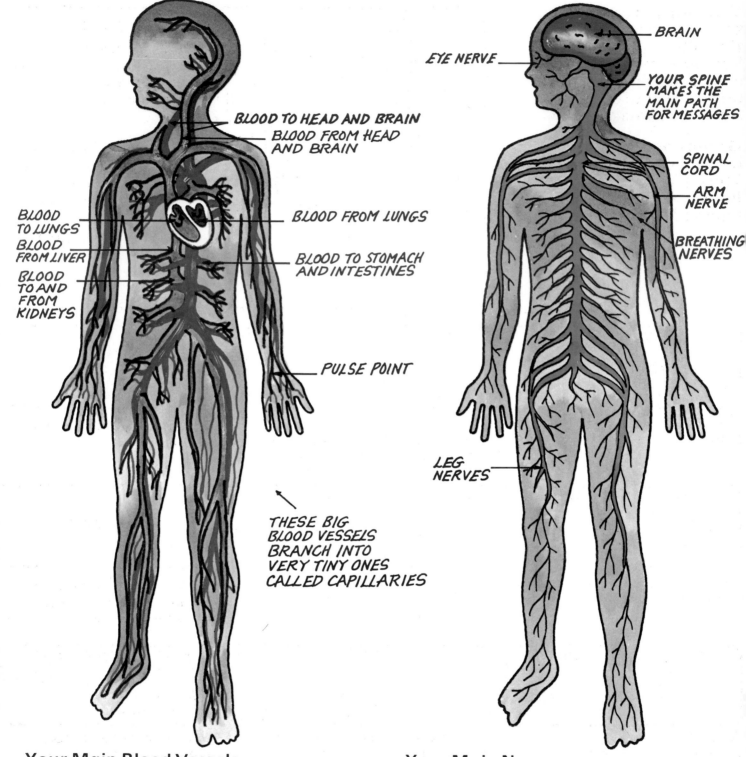

BLOOD TO HEAD AND BRAIN
BLOOD FROM HEAD AND BRAIN

BLOOD TO LUNGS
BLOOD FROM LIVER
BLOOD TO AND FROM KIDNEYS

BLOOD FROM LUNGS

BLOOD TO STOMACH AND INTESTINES

PULSE POINT

THESE BIG BLOOD VESSELS BRANCH INTO VERY TINY ONES CALLED CAPILLARIES

EYE NERVE

BRAIN

YOUR SPINE MAKES THE MAIN PATH FOR MESSAGES

SPINAL CORD

ARM NERVE

BREATHING NERVES

LEG NERVES

Your Main Blood Vessels
Here we have shown the heart a little bigger than it really is, so that you can see how the blood goes through it. The blood vessels leading out are called arteries. The ones leading in are called veins.

Your Main Nerves
The main path for messages to your brain goes right through the middle of your backbone. The main nerves connect to it like this. Hundreds of tiny nerves join these big ones.

What are Bodies Made Of?

Your body, like all living things, is made of very tiny bits called cells. You have many kinds of cell. Each does a different kind of work. Here are some of them.

Groups of the same kind of cell are called tissue. The different parts of your body are made of different kinds of body tissue.

How Big is a Cell?

Most cells are so small that you would need a very strong microscope to see them. Try this to see how very small they are:

Peel off one of the layers of thick skin on an onion. Under it you will find a sort of thin tissue. This is just one cell thick. Feel it. It is so thin you can see through it.

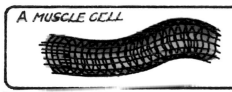
A MUSCLE CELL

This is a muscle cell. It can squeeze and stretch.

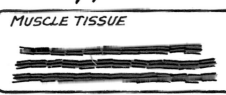
MUSCLE TISSUE

Muscle cells join into stringy bits called fibres. You can see them in meat. It is muscle tissue.

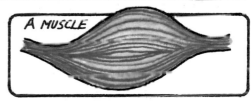
A MUSCLE

A muscle squeezes when all of its cells squeeze.

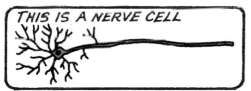
THIS IS A NERVE CELL

The long bits pick up and carry messages.

THIS IS A BUNDLE OF NERVE CELLS

Nerve cells join together into bundles, like wires in a telephone cable.

These bundles of nerves join the main cable in your spine that goes to your brain.

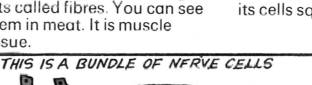
THESE ARE RED BLOOD CELLS

A drop of blood under a microscope shows cells like these floating in a colourless liquid.

RED BLOOD CELLS TRAVEL THROUGH YOUR BLOOD VESSELS

WHITE BLOOD CELLS

RED BLOOD CELLS

BODY CELLS

Red blood cells carry oxygen to other body cells. The liquid part of your blood carries bits of food.

All of your cells need food and oxygen to stay alive and do their work.

THESE ARE SKIN CELLS

Only the bottom layer of cells is alive. It makes new cells and pushes them up.

A CELL GROWS LIKE THIS

This picture shows how a new cell is made. We have coloured the growing skin cell red.

See how the cell swells and stretches until it breaks into two cells.

Body Words

Eating Words

Oesophagus – the food pipe that goes to your stomach.
Epiglottis – a flap of gristle behind your tongue that stops food going down your windpipe.
Carbohydrates – foods such as bread and potatoes that give you energy.
Proteins – foods such as meat, eggs and cheese that make muscle.
Fats – foods such as butter and oil that give you energy.
Vitamins – important things in food that keep you healthy.
Abdomen – the part of your body under your chest where your stomach and intestines are.
Bladder – the bag that stores waste water.
Anus – the hole where solid waste goes out of your body.
Faeces – undigested food (solid waste) that goes out of your body through your anus.
Urine – a mixture of water and waste taken from your blood by your kidneys. It is stored in your bladder until it goes out of your body.

Breathing Words

Larynx – the part of your windpipe that holds your vocal cords.
Trachea – your windpipe.
Lungs – the two air bags in your chest you use for breathing.
Bronchial Tubes – the tubes that lead from your windpipe to your lungs.
Diaphragm – the sheet of muscle between your lungs and your stomach that helps you to breathe.

Blood and Heart Words

Blood Vessel – a tube that carries blood.
Vein – a blood vessel that carries blood to your heart.
Artery – a blood vessel that takes blood from your heart.
Capillary – a very tiny blood vessel that brings supplies to the cells and takes away waste.
Antibody – a special weapon made by the blood to fight germs.
Plasma – the watery liquid part of the blood.

Bone, Muscle and Skin Words

Spine – your backbone.
Vertebra – one of the bones that make up your backbone.
Cartilage – gristle, which is a bit like bendy bone.
Tendon – a tough, stringy bit that connects muscle to bone.
Joint – where two bones link up.

Baby-Making Words

Puberty – the time when the baby-making machinery starts working in a girl or boy.
Ovaries – the part of a girl's body that stores eggs.
Testicle – the part of a boy's body that makes and stores sperm.
Ovum – the egg cell in a girl's body that becomes a baby when it is fertilized.
Sperm – the special cells made by a boy's testicles that can fertilize egg cells.
Penis – the part of a boy that lets out urine and sperm.
Uterus – the part of a girl where an unborn baby grows.

Fertilization – the joining of an egg and a sperm to start making a baby.
Menstruation – the clearing out of the uterus each month if a baby does not start.
Placenta – the cushiony lining of the uterus that brings food to an unborn baby and takes away waste.
Umbilical cord – the tube that connects the placenta to the unborn baby.

General Words

Nerves – tiny threads that carry messages to and from your brain.
Cell – the very tiny bits all living things are made of.
Tissue – a group of cells that look and act the same, such as muscle tissue.
Organ – a group of cells that work together to do a special job. Your heart is an organ.
System – a group of organs that work together. Your heart and blood vessels together make up your blood system.

Index